Weekly Reader Books presents

JELLY
and the
SPACEBOAT

by SHIRLEY PARENTEAU

with illustrations by
BLANCHE L. SIMS

Coward, McCann & Geoghegan, Inc.　　　New York

For my husband, Bill, captain of our family's cruises through the Sacramento Delta.

Text copyright © 1981 by Shirley Parenteau
Illustrations copyright © 1981 by Blanche L. Sims
All rights reserved. This book, or parts thereof,
may not be reproduced in any form without permission
in writing from the publishers. Published simultaneously
in Canada by Academic Press Canada Limited, Toronto.
Library of Congress Cataloging in Publication Data
Parenteau, Shirley.
Jelly and the spaceboat.
Summary: Jelly and Rich find themselves headed down
the Sacramento River on an unusual houseboat with a
crew from outer space.
[1. Sacramento River—Fiction.   2. Extraterrestrial
beings—Fiction.   3. Science fiction] I. Sims, Blanche.
II. Title.
PZ7.P2167Je   [Fic]   81-347
ISBN 0-698-20514-6   AACR1
First printing
Designed by Catherine Stock
Printed in the United States of America

One

Jelly squooshed her toes into the soft rich mud of the Sacramento River Delta. Cold, murky water came almost to the shirttails that hung over her cut-off jeans, but the first rays of morning sunlight were warm against her back. The line from her pole disappeared in the water ahead of her.

The city kid sat on a log nearby, keeping his leather Adidas dry. He was talking about San Francisco, again. Everything was better in San Francisco, he said.

Jelly's bare toes touched the hard round shell of a clam buried in the mud. She caught the clam between the crook of her toes and the pad of her foot and pulled it slowly up through the mud and water and into her fingers.

"The food is better," the city kid was saying. "The air smells better. Even the clouds look better in San Francisco."

Jelly braced her pole under her arm and worked on the clam's hinges with her pocketknife. The blade rasped against the rough shell. *A little pressure here*, she thought, catching her tongue between her teeth. *The right aim there....* Clam juice spurted out.

It caught the city kid as he was saying, "San Francisco can't be more than sixty miles down the river, but it might as well be on the moon." He jumped when the clam juice hit him, then he sputtered and wiped his face.

Jelly doubled over laughing. "Oops," she said, when she could get the words out. "On the Delta, we sometimes make mistakes."

"That wasn't a mistake, Jill-Ann Mason." He looked angry, but Jelly wasn't worried. She might be only eleven to his fourteen, but she was a "river rat," born and raised on the Delta. She could outrun him easily. And she knew the fields and sloughs like a catfish knows the currents.

"Maybe it wasn't a mistake," she told him. "Maybe that clam knew how sick I was of hearing about San Francisco. Listen, Rich, it was my unlucky day when you moved next door. My mother just had to take pity on you. 'Show Rich around, Jelly. Make him feel at home.' As if my Sundays were so empty I needed help filling them."

"This isn't any holiday for me, either," he muttered. "In the city, I could be checking out Fisherman's Wharf with my pals."

Jelly put her hands on her hips. "If you like San Francisco so much better, why don't you go back there?"

"I wish I could." He pulled his line from the water and looked at the bait clam dripping on the hook. "Ugh."

An idea began to light up the back of Jelly's mind. "Maybe you can. Unless you're chicken."

His head jerked around. "Nobody calls me chicken."

4

"Let's go, then. You can show me all around this terrific city of yours, where the food and air and clouds and everything are so much better."

"What are you talking about? Swimming down the river? It wouldn't surprise me to learn you river rats have gills. But I don't."

"I don't need gills. I helped my brother, Jay, study charts of the Delta and San Francisco Bay when he got his cruiser. He says I have a photographic memory."

"So?"

"So I know where boaters are headed, even when they're back in the Delta sloughs. Look out there, Rich." She waved her hand toward the river. Morning sunlight glimmered across the silken billowing water and sparkled from wave tips.

It also sparkled from the windows of two white cruisers and a bright blue houseboat that were plowing their way down-river, a few yards offshore. Their wakes swelled behind in a spreading trail that now began washing against Jelly's legs and thudding against the bank below Rich.

"Lots of boats come up here for the weekend," Jelly said. "Now they're heading back. And we can go with them."

"How?"

"Easy. We hide aboard for a free ride downriver."

"That's crazy."

She reeled in her line and picked a bit of rubbery clam from the hook. "You're chicken, all right. I thought so."

He was silent for a long moment. Then he jerked the clam off his own hook and hurled it into the water. "You haven't really got the nerve," he said. "But I'm curious to see just how far you'll go with this joke."

"Come on, then. Before they all leave their moorings in The Meadows."

She laughed to herself as Rich followed her across the road

and down a steep levee bank into a pear orchard. The Meadows Slough was about half a mile away. It was a quiet tree-lined arm of water where boaters liked to anchor. A narrow brushy channel led from The Meadows to another slough that wound south, joining other waterways before reaching the river several miles downstream.

The Meadows was a favorite with boaters, Jelly reminded herself silently. Best of all, it was where her brother had moored his cruiser for the weekend. Jelly knew he planned to head for San Francisco Bay after breakfast. It would be easy to hide Rich and herself aboard since Jay never went into the cabin before a cruise. He might be angry when she showed herself, but he'd get over it. And he could radio back to tell her mother and Rich's folks where they were.

Maybe she would tell Rich about her brother when the cruiser got underway. Maybe not. She hoped he would get seasick. That would show him city kids weren't as tough as river rats.

The soft black earth under their feet slowed their steps. "It's peat," she told Rich when he kicked at a clod. "A long time ago, it was underwater. There's no richer farming land any- where."

"Hold the lecture," Rich said quickly. "My folks already told me how the water was pumped out behind the levees, and how the farmland is lower than the river, and how great it is for tomatoes and asparagus and the rest. But it's like living in a giant maze."

"Hey, don't make any city-boy noise about the levees," Jelly said. "Just be thankful they're there. Or maybe you'd like to have your house wash away when the river floods."

Rich raised a hand to stop her words. "Excuse me, Miss Delta-breath. I keep forgetting you're hooked on river his- tory."

"And proud of it." Jelly gave him her most syrupy smile, the one she saved for people who tried to straighten her collar or tuck in her shirt. She ran ahead of him across the grassy field above The Meadows Slough, then looked along the bank for her brother's cruiser.

Jay's boat was just leaving the tree-lined waterway. Its wake rolled gently back against the bank with sad lapping sounds. Jelly felt her smile fade.

"Well," Rich said. "Which one do we take?"

She glanced at him, then at the boats still moored along the bank. Her cheeks felt hot. If she backed down now, Rich would never let her hear the end of it. She had to think of a way out. Maybe she could work it so that Rich would be the one who backed down. He didn't really want to stow away. She kicked through the damp grass, thinking hard.

"Come on, come on," Rich said, following her. "Make up your mind."

Pretty sure of yourself, aren't you? she asked him silently, as they rounded the hook-like end of the slough. She stopped so suddenly Rich almost walked into her. Floating against the bank was the craziest-looking houseboat she had ever seen.

Metal posts connected wooden pontoons to each side of a narrow wood hull. Above the hull, black-painted walls sloped outward. At about head-height, they met a wood-shingled roof, which slanted down from a high peak. The bow was six-sided, and pointed like a diamond. But the weirdest part was the windows. They were scattered across the roof and the walls, some with colored panes, and many with white-painted sashes.

"Wow," Rich said. "Somebody raided a junkyard and stuck everything together to make a boat."

Jelly walked to the edge of a wooden gangplank. It stretched from the levee side to a black door in the middle of the overhanging wall. No crew was in sight. Curiosity made her skin tingle.

"Let's look inside," she said.

"Not me. That thing looks ready to sink."

She had him! A feeling of joy rushed through Jelly. She had to bite her tongue to keep from laughing. She would insist they hide aboard this boat or none of them. But first, she wanted to see more of the crazy-looking thing.

"You *are* chicken," she whispered so he would remember afterward that he was the one who backed down. Then she stepped onto the gangplank. It squeaked against the muddy bank and swayed under her feet as she tiptoed across.

The black door slanted above her head. She put her ear close, but couldn't hear anything. She glanced back at Rich, then pushed.

The door was hinged at the top. It swung silently inward. Jelly held it above her head and peered into a narrow hallway. The floor was a good three feet below the opening. There were no stairs. After a wave to Rich, she jumped.

Two

Inside the boat, Jelly landed catlike on her fingers and toes, ready to scramble back through the doorway if anyone appeared. But the boat was silent except for the sound of creaking wood as it shifted on the water. Meadowlarks sang from cottonwoods along the bank.

The boat shifted again as Rich stepped on the gangplank. Jelly straightened as he pushed the door open. "I know I'm crazy," he whispered. "but my mom would skin me if I let you walk into trouble alone."

Timbers creaked again. Just the natural movement of the boat, Jelly thought. She was listening so hard her ears hurt, but all she could hear was the meadowlarks and the creaking wood.

The entryway was dim, but her eyes were adjusting. She felt

her uneasiness fade and her curiosity come back. She let out her breath and grinned at Rich.

"It's only a boat," she told him. "Crazy on the outside, but still only a boat. Looks to me like it was built on an old Army landing barge."

He was leaning over a waist-high partition to the right. "Would you call this a galley?"

She crowded beside him in the narrow passage. Ahead was a large kitchen with white stove and refrigerator. Wide windows with clear glass panes rose over a waist-high tiled counter. Beyond a sliding glass door, Jelly glimpsed a wooden stern deck. Under the overhanging trees of the slough, the galley looked almost as dim as the entry.

Jelly leaned farther across the partition. "There's something funny about the controls on that stove."

"There's something funny about this whole boat," Rich said. "Look how dim the galley is. It's not just because of the trees. It's the glass, too. I never saw windows with such heavy glass. Come on, Goldilocks. Let's get out of here before the Three Bears get home."

"I've seen a lot of strange things come up here from the city," Jelly said, pausing to be sure he knew she included him. "But this is the strangest. Let's just take a quick look around."

Rich sighed loudly, but she pushed past him and climbed a second half-wall toward the bow.

"Wow," she whispered, and motioned to Rich to look with her. The forward end of the boat was a large open room with a round oak dining table in the center. Wood chairs of several sizes and shapes were scattered around. But it was the huge, many-paned windows sloping over the water to shape the diamond-pointed bow that held Jelly's eyes. Glass prisms dangled over the panes, scattering color across the floor wherever sunlight reached them through the trees.

There was no sign of a crew. Jelly turned to Rich, feeling faintly disappointed. "Nobody home."

"So, we're lucky," he said. "Let's get out."

Although the boat seemed deserted, Jelly hesitated. She knew her mother would say her "curiosity bumps" were blocking her usual good sense. But she swung her legs over the partition and tiptoed into the room. She could see water in the slough gleaming below the lower bow windows.

Open lofts reached in from each side of the high ceiling. Jelly watched a stiffly inflated porcupine fish swing from a line fastened to the peak.

"I wonder what's in the lofts," she murmured. "I don't see any ladders."

Suddenly, a girl's head appeared at the edge of one loft. Long blond hair fell across her cheeks. A beaded headband held it from her forehead.

"Hey, wow!" she said. "Company."

"Crazy!" That was a man's voice, from the other loft. Jelly spun and found herself staring up at a bearded man with long brown hair, dressed in fringed buckskin.

"Peace." Jelly whirled back. The girl was now beside her shoulder and offering her a white daisy on a long stem.

She sure got down fast, Jelly thought, feeling scared but still curious. She took the flower and tried to smile, glancing about for a climbing rope, but not seeing any. Her "curiosity bumps" were changing into darts of alarm.

When you know you're where you shouldn't be, you'd better make your smile a good one, she told herself, and forced the corners of her mouth even higher as she turned back to the blonde. "Nice boat you have."

The girl looked puzzled. "Nice?" she repeated. "The boat is nice?" She sounded like someone repeating phrases from a foreign-language guide and unable to find the meaning.

"It's groovy," Rich said from the entry.

Jelly gave him a startled look, then saw he was waiting for a response from the blonde. The girl's face brightened as if she'd found someone who spoke her language.

"Groovy!" she cried. She glided to Rich without seeming to touch the floor, and handed him a daisy.

Score one for the city kid, Jelly thought, then added aloud, "She's light as a feather. What is this, anyway? A boat full of hip magicians?"

"How long have you been back here, Feather?" Rich asked the girl. "Flower children went out of style way back in the Sixties. Even on Fisherman's Wharf."

Two more heads peered down from the first loft. One was a girl with a cloud of black hair. Bright red hearts were painted on her cheeks. The other was a red-haired man whose round beard and frizzy hair ran together so that Jelly couldn't tell where one began and the other stopped.

"Out of style?" the girl called. "How can we be out of style? We studied the tapes. Do you mean we are not typical Earth people of this date?"

"That's a strange way to put it," Jelly said carefully.

"Quiet, Love," said the man. Squeaking as if pinched, Love ducked back into the loft.

The girl Rich called Feather touched Jelly's cut-off jeans with her fingertip. "Hippie?" she asked, sounding hopeful.

Jelly shook her head and raised her chin high. "River rat. And proud of it."

"Is this boat going to San Francisco?" Rich broke in.

The four stared eagerly toward him. "Do you know the way?" asked the man in buckskin.

Rich pointed at Jelly. "She's a walking river chart."

"Groovy," they shouted.

"But we thought you came from the city," Rich went on.

smiles. "We started for it but we got lost," said Feather. "It's all weeds and water and trees here. And every channel looks like the one before it."

Started from where? Jelly wondered. If this weird boat came down the river, she would have known about it. Deciding this was no time to ask questions, she pictured her brother's chart in her mind.

"You're northeast of San Francisco," she said, "near the top of the Delta. It's a marshy sort of place with about 20 by 45 square miles of farmland and water. Two rivers run through on their way to the Pacific Ocean. You won't find a prettier place anywhere."

"This mess of rivers, sloughs, levees, marshes, and old river channels is home to her, as you may have guessed," Rich said, nodding at Jelly. He grinned at the girl called Love, who was now standing beside him. "The City's home to me. We'll be happy to guide you there."

Jelly gave him a second startled look. Wasn't he the one who wanted to get off the boat just a few minutes ago? She didn't want to go anywhere with this group. But Rich looked as happy as a clam.

A motor thrummed to sudden life. Jelly felt the boat shiver under her feet. "What's that?" she cried.

Rich pointed through the entry hall. The red-bearded man was in the galley, working controls on the stove. *I was right,* Jelly thought. *There is something funny about that stove.* "How did he get back there so fast?" she asked.

Rich shrugged, but his eyes were bright with excitement.

The gangplank slammed shut against the side. The boat shuddered. Jelly braced her feet as it swung away from the bank and pointed down the slough past the remaining moored boats. The water rippled to either side as they turned down a channel no wider than her bedroom at home.

Blackberry bushes came close to brushing the wide sides of the houseboat, but Jelly didn't notice. A speedboat was rushing down the slough, traveling at full speed toward their diamond-pointed bow.

"Look out!" Jelly screamed, and threw herself flat. The roar of the speedboat swamped all other sound.

Three

The boat lifted like an elevator. Jelly saw the tops of trees. The engine roar of the speedboat seemed to be everywhere. Then the boat dropped. Water splashed up the bow windows and fell back in a sparkling sheet.

Jelly stared wide-eyed through the bow as the water fell away. The slough was clear. The speedboat was gone. She could still hear the engine, but the sound was fading.

Rich tugged her arm. She got to her feet and looked through the entry and galley to the stern windows. There was the speedboat, rushing on down the slough toward The Meadows. People inside pointed back and waved excitedly.

While she watched, the speedboat left the slough, careened up and over the bank and stopped in a blackberry tangle.

"Jelly," Rich said. "This is no ordinary boat."

She had trouble finding her voice. "Gee," she said finally. "You city kids sure can figure things out."

A voice shouted from the slough ahead. The boat moved past too soon for Jelly to see the trouble, but she heard the shouting from alongside and then from the stern. She wasn't surprised to see a lone fisherman clinging to the side of a skiff beyond the stern windows. The smaller boat rocked back and forth in the houseboat's wake. When the fisherman let go of his boat to shake his fist, he almost fell overboard with the next wave. Brush whizzed by as the houseboat picked up speed.

Jelly knew there would be a lot of fishermen along the sloughs. She ran to the short wall and shouted into the kitchen. "Hey! You with the beard! Slow down when you pass a fisherman."

"A what?" Redbeard peered in at her.

Jelly drew a shaky breath. "A fisherman. Like that one you almost swamped. Boy, you don't know much about the Delta, do you?"

"Lucky you found us," said the man in buckskin. He was standing beside Jelly and grinning. "We'll keep you aboard."

Jelly felt her heart skip a beat. "Keep us aboard?" Her voice ended on a squeak.

"Relax," Rich told her. "How often do you get to ride around in a spaceship?"

There was a sudden silence. The four crew members looked at one another and back at Rich. "How did you know?" asked the man in buckskin.

Rich was looking smug again. But his eyes glittered with renewed excitement. "Things you've said. The way you move."

Spaceship, Jelly thought. *Could it be true?* She glanced again at the four. First city kids, now space people. The Delta sure was changing!

The four crew members were looking troubled. Something else nibbled at Jelly's thoughts. She turned toward the galley. "Are there more of you, or should somebody be steering this thing?"

"Whoops!" Redbeard slapped his forehead with his hand, then cleared the two half-walls without touching either and landed beside the stove in time to twirl a burner, turning the boat away from a bank. "I keep forgetting we don't have all of space around us," he called.

Rich and Jelly exchanged long looks.

"No, tell us," the blonde girl insisted. She pulled at Rich's sleeve. "How did you guess we weren't from Earth?"

"It's why he called you Feather," Jelly said. "We have to touch down with our feet when we move around."

The other three laughed, then clapped one another on the back. "Keep our feet down when we move," said the girl with the painted cheeks. "Groovy."

"You look and sound like San Francisco in the late Sixties," Rich said.

"Oh, right." The girl looked pleased. "We studied. One of our Scout ships took pictures and recordings then. When we knew we were coming here, we got them from our library and studied really hard."

"Things have changed," Rich said. "Even in San Francisco."

"So soon?" Feather's eyebrows raised. "That's not fair. It took a lot of work to get all this ready."

Love sat down on the floor with her feet tucked under her. She frowned so hard, the hearts painted on her face looked crooked. "Well, I'm not going through any more tapes. I worked hard on this assignment. And that's all I'm going to do."

"But that's just it," Jelly said. "Why did you work so

hard? Why are you here at all?"

"Yeah. Why not level with us? What are your plans?" Rich added.

The man in buckskin stared at his feet. "We're supposed to fit in with the natives. We have to make our base in a harbor near San Francisco."

"But we landed in the wrong place," said Feather. "We floated around all night. Every place looks like every other place. There are just too many channels and sloughs."

"Maybe you should stay lost," Jelly said. "How do we know you aren't planning something awful?"

Feather handed her another daisy. "Peace."

"We don't want flowers. We want answers," Jelly cried. "If you think I'm going to guide any bunch of alien invaders down to San Francisco, forget it. I don't want you in my Delta, but maybe it's the safest place. I hope you shrivel up and die back here. I'm going to swim ashore."

She ran for the galley, planning to dive from the deck in the stern. But when she lunged for the half-wall, the air above it was suddenly as solid as a door. She turned slowly and stared at the space crew.

"We don't mean any harm. Honest," said Feather.

"We're just here to study the animal life," Love added.

The man in buckskin looked embarrassed. "To tell you the truth, we're in trouble. We flunked our last assignment. That was on Alpha Centauri. If we mess up this time, we'll have to take the whole class over."

"It was your fault," Love told him angrily. "Mixing the zobs with the zans. Couldn't you see the zans had eyes?"

"Very little eyes," he snapped back.

Jelly stared. "You mean you're students?"

"Galactic U!" Feather began what could only be a team cheer. At the end, she shrieked, "Stars! Stars! Stars!" and leaped straight into the air. Her hair brushed the ceiling. She hovered there, smiling down at Jelly.

"So, will you help us get to San Francisco Bay? We need to reach a town nearby. It's called Sausalito."

Jelly pulled her eyes away from the blonde and turned to see who had asked the question. It was Redbeard. How long had he been standing beside her? And who was steering?

"My brother has friends in Sausalito," Jelly said, feeling numb.

But who was steering?

Before she could ask him, the boat crashed into the bank with a solid WHUMP! Jelly fell to her knees. Feather dropped from the ceiling and fell sprawled across her.

Four

Jelly raised her head and stared through the bow windows. There wasn't much to see, just a dark mass of cottonwood roots, blackberry vines and mud.

Love was laughing. Jelly untangled herself from the blonde and scrambled to her feet. "What's so funny?" she demanded.

"You," Love gasped. "You and your planet. What a funny way to plan your waterways, all full of bends and turns."

"You're the funny ones," Jelly said shortly. She went into the galley, following Rich and the men. They were trying the engine. Jelly felt the boat shiver, but it didn't move free of the bank.

She walked onto the stern deck and leaned over the side. The pontoons were rammed solidly into the mud exposed by the low tide.

"Looks like we'd better get out and push," Buckskin said from the doorway. He motioned to his crew. "Come along, friends."

Jelly crouched down on the deck. She watched the space crew climb carefully over the boat rail and into the mud. They weren't floating now. They had to sink to their knees in the ooze to get the force they needed to shove against the hull. Rich sat on the deck beside Jelly. "Aren't you going to help your friends?" she asked.

He grinned. "Me? I'm just along for the ride you promised me." He hugged his knees and leaned forward to watch the crew struggle with the boat.

"This can't be happening," Jelly said.

"Why not?" he asked, keeping his eyes on the crew. "Your little Delta mind doesn't stretch to take in spaceships, even when you ride in one? Is that it?"

"I might have known you would be a science freak," she yelped. "I just want to go home."

"You wanted to go to San Francisco a little while ago."

"Not on a flying saucer! And this one isn't even flying."

"That's right." Rich leaned closer to the deck edge. "Hey, Redbeard! Why don't you lift out of this with your rockets?"

The spaceman wiped his forehead with his arm, leaving a smear of good Delta mud across his skin and curly hair. "We can't. The rockets are trapped in this muck."

Rich looked even more interested. "The rockets . . . where are they, anyway?"

Jelly scowled. "Next thing I know, you'll be asking for a tour of their home planet and dragging me along." She bit her tongue, hoping she hadn't given Redbeard any ideas.

She needn't have worried. He looked embarrassed and shook his head so hard that splatters of dirt flew. "We can't take you there. It isn't permitted. And there isn't time. We have to be in San Francisco Bay by sundown."

Jelly breathed a quick sigh of relief. Then she thought about his words and frowned. "The Bay by sundown . . . or what?"

Redbeard set his shoulder against the hull and shoved. His voice was a grunt. "Or we have to do an extra study. Of Alaska."

"Alaska," Jelly repeated. Her mind clicked busily. *What if these space bumblers weren't the students they pretended to be? What if they wanted to reach Alaska? Weren't air defense bases there? And what about San Francisco Bay? What could they damage before they headed north? And after she guided them there, like a junior Benedict Arnold,* she thought furiously. *I won't do it.*

The puttering sound of a motorboat broke into her thoughts. She raised her head quickly as a fisherman in a shallow boat came around the bend.

He looked them over and grinned. "Stuck tighter than a barnacle on a ship's behind," he said cheerfully. "Might as well wait for high tide, folks."

Jelly lunged to her feet. "Hey, Mister! Will you give me a lift to the nearest road?" She saw the space crew look at her.

"Watch it," Rich warned.

But the fisherman called, "Sure thing," and steadied his skiff against the houseboat's hull.

Jelly held her chin high, ignoring the space crew, and marched to the edge of the deck. She swung onto the rail. And smacked into an invisible wall like the one she'd hit inside.

She rubbed her nose with one hand and her knee with the other. "Uh . . . never mind," she told the fisherman. Then, leaning against the force field, and hiding her hands with her body, she signaled frantically for the fisherman to go for help. But he gave her a puzzled look, shrugged, and puttered away.

Jelly slumped against the invisible wall and watched until

he turned a bend of the slough. As the sound of his motor faded, the force field disappeared. Jelly flopped overboard with a startled cry.

When she bobbed to the top, spitting water and rubbing her eyes, Redbeard was wading toward her.

"Take care, River Rat," he called. "We don't want to lose our guide."

Jelly tried to lunge away from him through the mud, but he caught her by the waist and boosted her toward the boat. She grabbed the stern rail, got a knee on deck, then hauled herself on board. Water streamed down her face and hair, and feelings of helplessness churned inside her.

Rich handed her his handkerchief. "Might as well enjoy the experience," he said cheerfully.

Jelly sighed and wiped her face. This was obviously a job for the Coast Guard. If she pretended to go along with the crew, maybe she could find a way to signal for help. "Listen, Redbeard," she called. "If we do get you to the Bay, will you let us go?"

"If you get us there in time. Otherwise, we'll need you to help us find Alaska."

"But I don't know the way to Alaska!"

"You're a smart girl," he said cheerfully. "You could find out for us."

Stay calm, Jelly told herself, then said aloud, "There's plenty of time. It's only about an eight hour cruise to the Bay. But you're stuck for now, like that fisherman said. You might as well come aboard and wait for high tide."

"Groovy!" Love hauled herself aboard, looking thankful.

"What's high tide?" asked the man in buckskin as he boosted Feather to the deck.

"They sent you to a harbor on the ocean and you don't know what tide is?" Jelly asked. Maybe they really were bumbling students. "What kind of school did you have, anyway?" she added, with a frown.

Feather pouted. "Maybe we missed a lesson. But you needn't act so smart. You wouldn't know about tide, either, if you didn't live here."

"I don't believe any of this." The words popped out of Jelly's mouth. "This thing couldn't have come through space. It would have burned up. I think you're a bunch of jokers. You hypnotized us into thinking the boat flew back there."

Feather sighed and walked to the cabin wall. She pulled the edge of a shingle away from the roof. Blue-gray metal gleamed beneath. "We glued all this outside stuff on when we got here. We had it in boxes." She rolled her eyes. "What a job!"

Jelly studied the boat with its sides slanting out from the base, then in again to the shingled peak. Maybe it *was* a flying saucer covered over.

Rich was explaining to the others. "The water will rise in the ocean as the tide comes in and that will raise the water level in all these sloughs. You should be floating free in an hour or so."

"Pretty good for a city kid," Jelly said, raising one eyebrow.

"The tide will get us free by noon, then," Redbeard said with a glance at the sky. The others cheered and the two men climbed aboard.

Jelly suddenly realized the girls were clean and dry. Before she could ask about it, Love turned a flat-nosed gun toward the men. A ray of light flickered over them, and then both men were clean and dry again.

Jelly stumbled to her feet. Trails of water dripped over her knees from the fringe of her cut-offs. She shivered and pushed wet hair out of her face. "I'm convinced. Will you please aim that thing at me?"

The light tickled when it glimmered around her. It made

Jelly think of the cold shiver you get when you climb into a very hot bath. Then it was gone. She saw that her shirt and cut-offs were dry.

"Too bad we didn't bring our poles," Rich said. "We could catch some fish."

"Sportfishing!" Buckskin clapped his hands. "I remember— we studied that custom." He ducked into the galley and came back with a gleaming tube. Leaning over the deck rail, he sighted down the instrument. "I can see them. There are a lot of fish swimming around below our hull."

He pressed something on the tube and a ray of violet light flashed from the end and shot through the water. When Buckskin pulled the tube up, the ray held four catfish, stuck through like shish kebabs. He turned off the light ray and the fish dropped onto the deck, flopped a few times and lay still. He turned back for more.

"HOLD IT, MISTER!" called a loud voice.

Jelly jumped to her feet. A River Patrol boat was heading for them. The officer stood at the wheel, shouting through a bull horn. "I don't know how you did that, Mister. But you'd better have a fishing license."

Five

Jelly recognized the game officer as a neighbor, and caught her breath. She glanced at his holster, then at the alien tube in the spaceman's hands. She knew who would win any contest between them. She forced herself to move to the deck edge. "Hello, Officer Manning."

"Jill-Ann Mason!" He lowered the bull horn. "What are you doing with this crew?" His glance took in the oddly made boat and the hippie outfits of the space crew. His expression said clearly what he thought of them.

"Visiting friends?" Her voice squeaked. She cleared her throat and said firmly, "Visiting friends."

"Friends." His glance took in the crew again, then came back to her. His mouth was a taut line. "Well, your friend had better have a license. Or I'll take in his rod and reel."

ed. "It isn't his gear,"

her elbow into Rich's
ch. Show him your

e she said, sir. I'm . . .
loesn't it?"
anded it back. "Just

e from Buckskin. He
s I haven't got all the
You must have thick

ng making a mental
he patrol boat moved
to face Jelly. "Fast

s wake melted away
ity tongue would get

't you ask the officer

ing again, forking up
think I wanted to see
e had been on a Coast
we don't know what
I don't want to find
home."
said. "Looks like he's
."
h already flopped by
ewer-full on the pile.

The other crew members cheered and clapped their hands.

"Listen, Buckskin," Jelly cried. "We only want enough to eat. We're not running a cannery here."

Feather wrinkled her nose. "How can you eat these?"

"First, you have to clean them." Jelly looked around the group. "Any volunteers?"

"You're the river rat," Rich said cheerfully. "And proud of it, as I remember. I've never cleaned a fish in my life."

Jelly sighed and pulled out her pocketknife. It was clear that arguments would not get her off this boat. She would have to make the best of it—pretend to go along and keep her eyes open for a chance to escape.

She sat cross-legged by the pile of fish and got to work.

Love clapped her hands over her mouth. Her dark eyes were wide. "You're pulling off the skin!"

"That's the way to get catfish ready to eat," Jelly said. She cut a skinned catfish from stem to stern and tossed the entrails overboard. "Want to help?"

"Yuck! No!" Love backed away so fast, she hit the rail and nearly went overboard herself.

"You're kidding us, aren't you?" Buckskin asked. He looked slightly pale. "You don't really eat those things."

"No, we wear them for shoes." Jelly could see her sarcasm went over his head. "What do you eat?" she asked.

"Food."

"Oh, yes? Clever of you." Jelly raised an eyebrow at Rich and reached for another catfish, careful to keep her fingers away from the thornlike spines on its fins.

"Food?" Rich asked. "Can you tell us more than that?"

"Food comes in lots of flavors and colors," the blonde said. "It's in crunchy cubes and packed in a box."

"How very civilized," Jelly said sweetly. She pointed a limp skinned catfish at Rich. "Sounds like your kind of people."

He ignored her. "Why haven't you brought your own food along?"

"We couldn't." Buckskin scratched his forehead under the headband. "Native food is part of our studies."

Love gulped. "But they didn't tell us it would look like *that,*" she said in a muffled voice.

Jelly turned to Buckskin. "Part of your studies for what?"

"To learn how you people live," he said and sighed. "We wanted to go to Aldebaran. But no, they sent us to Earth."

"And that's bad?" Rich asked.

"Well, it isn't good," Feather said. She jerked her foot away from a catfish that had flopped loose from the pile. "How would you like to be assigned to a primitive planet?"

"It was his fault for mixing up the zobs and zans." Love frowned at Buckskin. " 'Prove you can do a simple assignment,' they said. 'Then you'll get a more interesting one.' "

Jelly jerked to her feet. "Let's see you do your simple assignment, then. Clean your own fish."

"But that's not food," Redbeard said.

"It is on simple Earth." Jelly felt her cheeks get hot.

The crew whispered together. She heard them mutter, "Primitive emotion," and felt her cheeks blaze even hotter. Rich touched her arm. "Easy, Jill."

She forced herself to calm down. Rich was right. They had to get this crew to the Bay by sundown or they would be shanghaied to Alaska. Unless they could sneak off the boat sooner. And she was going to try, whether Rich was with her or not.

"I thought *you* were strange," Rich murmured with a grin. "Compared to them, you're almost normal."

"Normal!" She hushed her voice, though she wanted to shout. "I'm alone in a crowd of weirdos. And I *do* include *you.*"

"Me! Why me?"

"You like this bunch."

He laughed. "I'll admit your muddy river Delta beats the city for fun, this time."

"Don't start that again," Jelly warned. But his teasing had taken the edge from her anger. She couldn't help smiling. She decided she might as well finish cleaning the fish.

Before she could move, one of the girls screamed. The rest of the crew began shouting. Jelly whirled around. She saw that Buckskin had been fishing again.

An eight-foot sturgeon whipped back and forth on the deck, like a beached sea monster. Its lean, ridged back gleamed like armorplate. The fish arched and flopped over the deck. Its small red eyes peered above the catfish-like whiskers. Cold river water ran from the fish, forming pools around Jelly's bare feet.

Six

Buckskin balanced on the deck rail, yelling, "Monster!" The women, still screaming, zipped upward like twin arrows. Jelly started to laugh. "I thought space travelers like you were used to all kinds of life."

Only Redbeard had stayed in place. His eyes were round and looked even bluer in the frizzy frame of his hair. "Groovy," he said, drawing the word out on a long breath. "More Earth food?"

"Some people like it," Jelly said, trying to look casual while pressing herself flat against the houseboat wall to avoid the twisting sturgeon.

The fish arched its body and flipped again. Its long thin tail swept out. It caught the pile of catfish and sent them all slithering across the deck and back into the slough.

"Looks like we'd better all learn to like sturgeon, if we're going to eat," Rich said. "Do you know how to clean that thing, Jill?"

He looked amused. Jelly gave him a cool look to match his own. "Sure," she said. "Just hand me my stone ax."

He laughed, then put his arm across her shoulders. "Come on, Jelly. They didn't mean to hurt your primitive Earth feelings."

She gave him her best imitation of an ape, with her teeth bared, her back hunched and her hands dangling below her knees. But not for long. The sturgeon made a last desperate lunge. Its tail brushed Jelly's toes as the fish slid across the deck and over the side. Water splashed back. The fish was gone.

Jelly dropped to the deck and rubbed her hands over her toes to get rid of the wet, cold feel of the fish. She couldn't help giggling. "See, Rich. We have fun like this all the time in the Delta."

"No more food," Feather said, as she and Love drifted to the deck. They did not look sorry to see the fish go.

Suddenly, the boat jiggled.

"The monster is attacking!" Buckskin shouted. The space women clung together.

"It's the tide moving in," Rich said. "We're starting to float free."

The boat jiggled again. This time, the crew cheered. Jelly sat where she was, studying the three feet of clear space between the deck and the rail. First the catfish, then the sturgeon had slipped over the side. Could she follow them? She edged closer to the rail.

Redbeard gunned the motor as the boat shifted on the rising water. Jelly felt the hull come free of the mud. The motor roared and they lurched ahead into the channel.

Jelly dangled her legs over the side, letting the water spray in crystal droplets over her toes.

Now, she thought. Dive clear of the boat! She threw herself under the rail. And landed hard against the force field. This time, it was like an invisible rubber wall. It let her swing out over the water, hang for an instant, then bounce back under the rail and onto the deck.

"Hey, River Rat," Buckskin said. "You almost fell overboard again."

Jelly sat up and rubbed her head. She knew he had been watching her all the time. "I'll have to be more careful," she told him, and added silently, *more careful I don't get caught.*

"Where do we turn, River Rat?" Redbeard called from the stove.

"My name is Jelly," she said stiffly. She got to her feet and walked inside to point out the turn from the narrow channel into Snodgrass Slough, a waterway that was only a little wider and lined with low islands covered with tule reeds.

Jelly stayed beside Redbeard as they traveled, pointing out underwater shoals and guiding the boat around the deep side of the tule islands. She concentrated hard on her memory of water depths marked on her brother's Delta charts. She kept her fingers crossed, hoping she wouldn't make a mistake and run them aground again.

The slough widened, but the tule islands were still a danger. Jelly was glad when they turned a bend that brought them into a river fork. The new waterway was about the size of a two-lane road, but she knew the river would grow broader as they traveled downstream.

They passed old rotting docks where pilings had sprouted branches. Cottonwoods and willows hung over the levee banks. The water was clear and still and reflected the trees perfectly; the boat seemed to float on air.

Jelly walked back to the deck to enjoy the cruise. Traveling through the Delta always made her feel good. For the first time, she was glad to be aboard the spaceboat. She smiled at Rich, ready to share the Delta's special beauty.

"Boy, how do you stand it?" he asked curiously. "Nothing but reeds and mud and levee banks. What your Delta needs is a lot of good solid sidewalks."

"Sidewalks!" Jelly yelped. "And a fast-food place on every tule island? Rich, you just don't understand. These waterways are historic frontiers."

"Oh sure," he said with a grin. "Frontiers."

"That's right. The Delta had brave steamboat captains and pioneer farmers and daring explorers. Not a bunch of money-hungry cutthroats, like in San Francisco."

Rich laughed: "Farmers! You wouldn't know a historic frontier if you walked into one."

"Oh yes I would," Jelly shot back. "I'm looking at one now." She pointed to a row of tule reeds. "That's color, Rich. That's history. You don't put sidewalks on history."

"Maybe the tules are your answer," Rich said, still grinning. "Build yourself a raft and float away from this crew."

"Maybe that's just what I'll do," Jelly said. "But I'm not sure I'll let you come along." She called back to Redbeard as the spaceboat picked up speed. "We'll be joining a big river called the San Joaquin in a little while, then into Rio Vista Bay."

"But we want San Francisco Bay," Redbeard said.

"I'm taking you there." Jelly shivered a little, wondering again just who she was taking to San Francisco, and what was really planned. Would she be able to help? Or was she to be a Benedict Arnold, after all?

What a way to get my name in the history books, she thought. Then she shook the worry away and turned again to the spaceman. "Rio Vista is on the Sacramento River. We'll follow the river to San Francisco." *And somewhere along the way*, she added silently, *I am getting off this tub.*

"Look at that bit of colorful history," Rich said, his voice teasing. "An old dock to nowhere."

"It went somewhere in its time," Jelly said as the boat passed a row of rotting pilings. "I just wish I'd lived here when the store ship came up the river. It would have been like a carnival."

She sighed and leaned against the rail, gazing after the pilings. "Farmers trading pigs and stuff. And the captain trading them salt or whatever. You talk about colorful, Rich. I wish I'd lived then."

"Pigs," Rich said. "Ugh."

She didn't speak to him again until they joined the San Joaquin River, and then only to point out a water shortcut through Three Mile Slough.

They came from the slough into rougher open water. Rio Vista Bay was filled with sailboats, the white sails puffing like fat pillows. They seemed almost to float above the water as they silently crisscrossed the Bay, tacking with the wind.

"How beautiful," said Feather. "Let's go closer."

"No!" Jelly cried. "Sailboats depend on the wind. They have the right of way over powered boats. Don't get in their path."

No one was listening. The spaceboat lumbered into the Bay with the crew leaning far over the deck rails, waving.

Sails dipped wildly as the boats tried to turn from their path. The spaceboat plowed on into their midst. Jelly groaned and covered her face with her hands.

"There's a pretty one," called Love. "Go that way, Redbeard."

"No!" Jelly yelped uselessly. The spaceboat headed across the Bay. A sail flipped around and pulled a boat over. Its owner clung to the keelboard, waving his fist and shouting.

38

There was a lot more shouting as the spaceboat bumbled on, and a lot more fists were raised. Someone spotted Jelly and shouted, "What's wrong with you, Jill-Ann Mason? Get your wild friends out of here."

Jelly wished she could sink to the bottom of the Bay. Careening boats and shouting boaters were on every side. Another sail went over. Redbeard and the crew paid no attention. Rich looked dumbfounded.

"Let's go that way," Feather shouted.

"No, that way," called Love.

Jelly remembered worrying that Officer Manning would report her weird friends to her mother. When word of this disaster got around, she would be grounded for sure.

She saw that the sailboats were now moving to the sides of the Bay to leave a clear channel. Redbeard finally swung the spaceboat around and headed again toward San Francisco.

Jelly sighed with relief. Grounded or otherwise, she was going to stay clear of marinas until this day was forgotten.

"I think we're in trouble," Redbeard said.

Jelly looked through the boat and out the bow windows. An enormous freighter was bearing directly toward them in the river channel. It was so near, she could see only the dark hull looming through the windows.

Seven

Now, she knew why the sails gave way. She clutched the door frame. "Redbeard, get us out of here!"

He yanked on the front stove burner, wrenching it hard right as the freighter's whistle blared. Jelly covered her ears. She wanted to cover her eyes, but didn't dare.

The steel bow pushed a mountain of water ahead as the freighter moved upriver. In moments, the spaceboat cut into the edge of the swell. The smaller boat rocked crazily. Jelly grabbed the deck rail. The freighter was so near, she half-expected her fingers to scrape against the rough metal plates of the ship's hull.

Spray soaked her clothes and hair and streamed down her face. "Use your rockets," she yelled.

Redbeard jerked the oven handle and the spaceboat lifted.

The rocking stopped. The spray fell away. The smaller boat floated just above the water as it moved away from the freighter. Redbeard brought it down again close to a reed and cottonwood island. He mopped his forehead with his arm. "Sorry, River Rat. I forgot about the rockets."

Jelly looked through shallow water to the mud below. "You're too close to shore," she began. Before she could say any more, the freighter's passage began pulling the water away. It was like a bathtub drain. Within seconds, the spaceboat sat flat on the mud.

"What happened?" asked Feather.

"The ship pushes the water ahead as it moves," Jelly said quickly. "Remember that mound in front? But the wake will hit in a moment. Hang on!"

The freighter's whistle blasted a last time. It sounded like a laugh. The big ship moved upriver, a surge of water pushing on with it. Wake rolled from its stern, coming across the water in giant swells. The first one whacked into the spaceboat and sprayed up and over it. Jelly felt the little boat wash higher onto the island. Another wave hit, then a third.

The last waves rolled more gently, and soon the river was quiet.

"What *was* that?" asked Redbeard.

"Just a ship on its way to Sacramento," Jelly said. "We've joined the main river now. We'll probably meet a lot of ships."

"Do we have to?" Love asked faintly. Her hands shook as she aimed the drying ray at each of them in turn.

"Unless you fly," Rich told Love, looking as if he hoped the crew would agree.

"We can't do that," Buckskin said. "We're not supposed to use our rockets." He shuffled his feet uneasily. "We'll be marked way down if they learn we used them, after all. Rockets would look suspicious, you see."

"Even to our primitive minds," Jelly agreed. If Rich could stay cool, so could she. "You're stuck again, you know," she told Redbeard. "And it serves you right for running around those sailboats the way you did. I've never been so embarrassed in my whole entire life."

"You were on the other end, this time," Rich reminded her cheerfully. "You're always putting down anyone who wasn't born among the tules. But when those sailboaters spotted you, they put you down good. How did it feel?"

"That's just what I'd expect to hear from a city kid," Jelly said, wishing she could think of a better answer. She turned back to Redbeard. "How are you going to get away from this mud?"

"That's why we have you along," he said with a broad grin. "You're the one who knows all about the river. We're really lucky you came aboard. But do something fast, River Rat. We have to reach San Francisco Bay by sundown."

"You already told me. And please call me Jelly." She crossed the deck and looked down at the pontoons. One lay on the mud. Water covered the one nearest the river. "I suppose your rockets are in mud again."

"One is." Buckskin came to stand beside her. "You sure have strange waterways on your planet."

"I'd say we have strange visitors," Jelly snapped. She was still stinging from Rich's remark. If he and these space creeps didn't like the Delta, she wished they would get out of it and leave her alone.

"The tide's still coming in," Rich said thoughtfully. He leaned over the rail beside them. "It won't float this pontoon from the mud very soon, but it should raise that outer one."

"Will that help?" Feather asked hopefully.

"Those forbidden rockets of yours are in the pontoons, aren't they?"

Buckskin looked surprised. "You're as smart as she is."

"Smarter," Rich said. "And it seems to me, you'll have to use your engine again. Just enough to fire the outer pontoon and swing this other one around and out of the mud."

"Groovy!" cried Love. She threw her arms around him in a delighted hug. "We'll keep you both with us."

"Only as far as San Francisco," Rich reminded her, his face turning red as Love held him.

"Oh, right," the girl agreed.

Jelly gave Rich a long look. She didn't like the way the crew smiled with such innocent expressions. They must be hiding something. She wondered if Rich trusted them. He looked awfully pleased with the girl's hug. Jelly suddenly felt very much alone.

"While we're waiting for the tide to rise," she said, "there's more of our strange native food nearby. Is anyone hungry?"

"I am," Feather said, but she looked wary. "Where is the food? Is it dead or alive?"

"It's alive," Jelly said and grinned when Feather looked disgusted. "Sort of, anyway. It's berries." She pointed at blackberry bushes hanging over a low bank. Dark ripe fruit showed through the thorny, deep green leaves. "Let's wade ashore and pick some."

"Berries," Redbeard repeated. "I think we studied berries. Or was it apples?"

"It's almost the same thing," Jelly said. "Come on." She swung over the rail. This time there was no invisible barrier. She waded through ankle-deep water, with the others following.

The berry bushes rose higher than her head. Golden-yellow tule reeds clumped together beyond them, with green-leafed cottonwoods rising above. Jelly picked a fat berry and popped it into her mouth. The sweet warm juice spread over her tongue. She rolled her eyes. "Ummm. Go ahead. Try one."

The crew hesitated, but finally Love reached for a berry. She put it into her mouth carefully, as if ready to spit it out at first taste. Instead, she sighed with pleasure. "This is *food*."

The others reached for berries. Soon they were all eating the fruit as fast as they could pick it. Their mouths and fingers turned purple with the rich dark juice.

Jelly moved from one bush to another, picking the juiciest berries. She searched for more around the sides and back of a clump of bushes. She was out of sight of the crew when she caught Rich's eye. She motioned to him to follow her.

He seemed to understand, but he shook his head and went on picking berries.

Jelly motioned again, harder. Rich didn't pay any attention. She hesitated for just a moment longer. Then she made a face at Rich and moved farther behind the bush. When she was sure the space crew couldn't see her, she started to run.

Eight

There wasn't much room to run. Jelly fought through the bramble. Thorns caught at her shirt and cut-off jeans, and raked across her hands and bare legs. The hot noon sun burned down. The need to hurry pushed her, making the thorns seem to cling even harder.

She knew that a road followed the levee across the channel from the far side of the island. Once there, she would be safe to make her way home. And to report to the Coast Guard.

She pulled her shirt impatiently from the prickly clutch of still another blackberry vine. The plants seemed almost alive, as if determined to hold her prisoner for the space crew. Jelly sucked at a bleeding scratch across the back of her hand. She could be as stubborn as any plants, she told herself, and shouldered her way through to the slender white trunks of the cottonwoods.

Leaning against a tree, she gazed back toward the boat. She could see the shingled roof beyond the blackberry bramble, but not the crew. There was no sound of anyone following. She sighed. If Rich had any sense at all, he would slip away as she had.

More thorns and underbrush blocked the far side of the island. She moved through carefully, lifting the vines aside instead of shoving. Even so, she got plenty of thorns in her hair. She was untangling it when she heard someone whistling.

It was a cheerful, absentminded sort of whistle. She recognized "Three Blind Mice" and was fairly sure the whistler was not one of the space crew. She pushed through reeds, her feet sinking in mud with each step.

A tow-headed boy of about eight sat in a rowboat snugged up to the outer edge of the tule reeds. A fishing line dangled from a pole in his hand. Jelly could have shouted for joy.

He heard the reeds rustle and turned quickly. "Don't scare my fish."

Jelly dug in her pocket. "Forget the fish. I'll trade you my knife for a ride across to the levee road."

The boy tilted his head. "Let me see the knife."

She waded into the shallow water and mud and held the knife toward him.

The boy poled the skiff closer, then took the knife from Jelly and studied it, turning it over and opening and closing each blade. "Okay," he said finally.

Jelly glanced back at the island. Why didn't Rich show up? The way that weird bunch was gobbling berries, they wouldn't notice him leave. She wondered how she would explain to his mother when she got home without him.

"Get in," the boy said. He was holding the skiff steady with an oar stuck down into the mud.

Still Jelly hesitated. *What will I say when I'm asked about Rich?* she wondered. *That he's probably on his way to Alaska?* She glanced again at the island. Even a city kid should be able to find his way across that.

"If you changed your mind, can I keep the knife?" the boy demanded. "You already scared away the fish."

"Who's changed her mind?" Jelly grabbed the side of the boat and climbed aboard. The skiff swung under her weight, but she kept her balance and sat on the plank seat in back. The boy pulled up the oar and pushed away from the reeds.

The boat jerked forward with the boy's pull on the oars. Jelly watched him row and tried to put Rich out of her mind. *Think of the oars,* she told herself. *Listen to them clank against the iron locks. Watch the blades dip through the water.*

So why was she thinking of the way she felt when the sailboaters shook their fists and shouted? Probably because she knew she would feel even worse when everyone blamed her for losing Rich.

"That dummy," she said. But it was her fault that he was on the spaceboat in the first place.

The boy rested his oars and looked at her curiously. The bow cut through the water, still moving toward the high levee bank across the channel. "What dummy?" he asked.

"Me," she said and sighed. "I've changed my mind, after all. Take me back to the island."

"Why?"

"Never mind, why. Just turn this thing around."

"My mom told me not to say girls are nuts," he said. "But you're nuts." He watched her for a moment longer, then shrugged and dipped his oars, turning the skiff.

Jelly grinned. "This time, even your mom would probably say you're right." She stepped from the boat as soon as it reached the tule fringe. "Keep the knife, pal. And hang around for a while. I may be back with a friend."

"I'm not sitting here for long," he said. "I got fishing to do."

She agreed with a nod of her head, and waded toward the end of the island. She wasn't about to fight her way through the blackberries again, not even for Rich. Her legs still smarted from the scratches.

When she rounded the end of the tule island, she waded close to the reeds along the outer side. Finally, she peered through a last thick clump. Rich was sitting on the deck of the spaceboat. He looked up as she parted the tules.

"Welcome back," he shouted, waving.

"Dummy," she said. She let the tules fall back and waded toward the boat. "Couldn't you see I was hiding? Why didn't you leave when I did?"

He chose a blackberry from a pile by his knee and chewed it slowly. "Why did you come back?"

"Why do you think I came back?" She sat on the deck and shoved a handful of the berries into her mouth. "I came back for you, dummy. Look, Rich, there may still be time." She caught at his sleeve. "Let's go!"

He shook off her hand. "But, Jill-Ann, don't you understand? I don't want to leave. This is a chance to find out about space and people on other planets and everything. I've got thousands of questions to ask the crew."

"Questions! For this crew? You don't really think they know any answers, do you?"

"Come on, Jelly," he said. "You're still angry because they called you primitive. Why don't you try to look at this whole problem from their point of view?"

"Which point of view is that?" she asked. "The point of view of a bunch of lazy learners who just happen to be from outer space, or the point of view of a bunch of aliens who are here to destroy our world?"

"Destroy our world! You've been reading too many stories, Jill-Ann."

"Maybe you haven't read enough! Or maybe you're blinded by a couple of hearts painted on a pretty face. Don't blame me when the disaster begins."

Rich was laughing again. That made her even angrier. Why couldn't she make him listen? She wished she had stayed in the rowboat. She'd given away a perfectly good pocketknife. And for what? To have Rich laugh at her. "I'm leaving," she said and swung her legs toward the edge of the deck.

But Buckskin called from the galley. "Hang on, River Rat. We're going to give it a try."

The rockets whooshed. Water sprayed back as the boat spun around. They were floating free again. The crew cheered. Jelly linked her arms around her knees. "We're on our way. Thanks to you."

"If I were stuck on their planet, I'd be glad of some help from the natives," Rich said.

"I don't mind helping if they're really harmless students, which I doubt. But I don't want to be a Benedict Arnold."

"You've got to learn to trust people, Jill. City kids and space people, and all."

"I don't know which is worse," she muttered. "And I don't want to make a long cruise to Alaska to find out."

Nine

Rich glanced at the sky, then at the riverbank whizzing past. "This boat's really picked up speed. We can reach the Bay by sundown, easily, if we don't have any more delays."

Love came from the galley and sat down beside Jelly. She held out her cupped hands. "Look what I found on the island, River Rat. Are these food?"

Jelly looked into Love's cupped palms. Four pale blue eggs nestled there.

"Robin's eggs," she said. "They're too small to be food. You should have left them in the nest."

"Eggs? Nest? What are those?" The girl's dark eyes looked wide and puzzled.

Jelly gave her a long look. "I sure wish you had paid more attention to your lessons."

Love peered at the eggs. She seemed to be searching her mind for an answer. "Eggs," she repeated softly. Suddenly, her eyes brightened. She turned to Jelly. "Eggs! I remember. A start of life."

"Very good," Jelly said. "Go to the head of the class."

But the girl looked troubled. She gazed again at the pale blue eggs in her hands. "Do you mean these are babies? I have taken some creature's babies?"

"Birds," Jelly said. She waved her hand toward a gull swooping overhead. "But not like that noisy thing. These would be smaller birds."

Love's face was filled with horror. "No! How awful! We must put them back into the nest." She hurried into the galley, holding the eggs carefully.

"Put them back," Jelly repeated. "Rich, we don't have time to turn back to the island. Or try to find that nest. Not if we're to reach the Bay by sundown."

He shrugged. "Alaska, here we come . . . and it's your fault, Jill-Ann Mason. You just can't resist showing off all you know about your muddy river Delta. Why didn't you tell her she was right, that she found some packaged food? She might even have liked the eggs, if you boiled them for her."

Jelly jumped up and followed the girl into the galley. She found Love showing the eggs to the others. Tears were running down her cheeks, blurring the painted hearts.

The space crew silently studied the eggs in Love's hands. Then Redbeard turned the stove timer. Jelly felt the boat slowing.

"You can't be serious," she cried. "We can't turn back to the island. If we're to reach the Bay by sundown, we can't lose any more time."

The crew turned together to stare at her. Their expressions said "primitive" more clearly than words. Jelly felt her own face get hot. They couldn't have looked more disgusted if she had suggested serving a pet goldfish for Sunday dinner.

"But they're just robin's eggs," she said.

"To keep these small eggs would be a waste of life," Buckskin told her.

This is crazy, Jelly told herself as Redbeard turned the spaceboat around. *They're being foolish. Why do I feel that I'm the one who is wrong?*

She shrugged and pulled her shoulders straighter, then walked stiffly back to Rich. She sat close beside him. "They're going to put the eggs back into the nest," she said quietly. "Maybe it's a good thing. Let them be late getting to the Bay. Maybe they won't be able to see where to put the bombs."

"Bombs!" Rich shouted. "You've got a one-track mind, Jill-Ann."

"Listen, Rich," she said urgently. She forced her voice to a whisper. "Listen to me. There's a boy with a boat on the other side of that island. While this space bunch is putting the eggs back into the nest, we can slip over the side. That boy is just waiting to help us escape."

Rich gave her a pained look. "I told you, Jelly. I don't want to escape."

"Well, I do," she cried. "How can I go without you?"

"Force yourself. Or stay aboard." He leaned against the cabin wall, looking pleased with himself. "I know what I'm going to do. I'm going along to San Francisco."

"And Alaska?"

He grinned. "Why not? I've never been to Alaska."

"Neither have I and I don't plan to go now." She rubbed her hands over the scratches on her legs and turned her head away from him. No use wasting any more good Delta breath on an argument with a fool.

They reached the tule island a short time later. The

spaceboat stayed clear of the mud this time, while Love floated over the side and above the tules. The others stood by a deck rail, watching.

Jelly glanced at Rich. Then she inched across the deck to the far rail and pushed her feet below it. The invisible barrier pushed back.

Rich grinned. "Looks like you missed your chance."

Redbeard turned to them. "Why are you frowning, River Rat? Are you worried about the time? We can go faster."

"Good," Jelly said with a sigh. "Just remember to slow down for small boats and marinas." *Especially Sausalito marinas,* she said to herself. *I may spot my brother's boat.*

"Okay, River Rat," the spaceman said cheerfully.

"That's not my name! Can't anybody around here say Jelly?" She knocked her forehead against the rail in frustration, while Rich laughed.

Love floated aboard, smiling. The others took her hands and patted her shoulders, laughing and smiling together.

"This is crazy," Jelly muttered. She heard the motor roar, then water sprayed back from the bow as the boat picked up speed.

Jelly's hair blew back as the spaceboat whizzed faster and faster down the river. They rounded a bend in a blur. She heard Redbeard whoop. Then they whizzed alongside and past a gleaming white freighter. The spaceboat rocked a little, settled back, and rushed on.

"Wow!" Rich called. "I hope there's nothing in our way."

"So do I," Jelly said. "I'm going to watch through the bow. Sitting back here and wondering is getting on my nerves."

Rich followed her through the boat to the window-filled bow. Feather was sitting at the oak table. She held a narrow gleaming tube and seemed to be using it to carve the wood. She looked up and smiled. "I'm making a report. I'm putting in that you have been kind and helpful."

"We primitives are like that," Jelly said, but she felt herself smile.

"I'm glad," the girl said. "I was a little bit afraid to come to this remote space area."

Jelly leaned across the table and looked straight into Feather's wide blue eyes. "You're not going to keep telling people that this is a primitive planet, are you?"

"Oh no. We have to pretend to be natives. We might have made some awful mistakes if we had not met you, River Rat. You have been so much help to us. We'll know how to fit in, now."

Jelly felt a twinge of warning. The words *junior Benedict Arnold* marched through her mind again. "Will you let us go when we reach the Bay?" she asked, frowning.

Feather hesitated. "Will we get there in time?"

"We will, at this speed," Rich said. He was standing by the bow windows. His voice sounded uncertain. Then he added, "I just hope we can keep it up."

Jelly crossed to the windows. The sun was low, but San Francisco Bay was not far ahead. The water spread wide now and was filled with wind-whipped waves. No wonder Rich had questioned the speed. Wisps of fog trailed around the edges of the river and floated above the surface, like billows of steam. In the distance, the sky was growing fuzzy as a white blanket rolled in from the sea.

The fog was the answer! Jelly knew it. She cradled the thought while she watched white mist build around them, soon muffling even the sound of the spaceboat's engine.

Ten

Jelly felt the spaceboat slow as the fog thickened. She walked back to the galley. "Can you see the channel?"

"No," Redbeard said. "Can you?"

"Not without a compass. Do you have one?" She held her breath, hiding her idea while she waited for his answer.

"Right here." He lifted the coffeepot to show that the back burner was a compass.

"Clever," she murmured.

"But I can only direct it to the stars," he said apologetically. "I don't know where to aim in the Bay."

"Another missed lesson?"

He grinned. "That's why we have you along."

"Lucky me," she said and bit back a smile of triumph. The idea was now a clear plan. In this fog, she could take them right to the Coast Guard dock.

"Remember," Redbeard said, as if he saw something of the idea in her face. "We want to go across from the city to a little town called Sausalito."

"And you report at sundown?"

Redbeard peered through the cottony fog. "We can report from anywhere in the Bay. Just to let them know we're in place, and on time. Then they'll let us know if we can stay or if we have to go on to Alaska."

Jelly shivered. She concentrated on watching the compass and matching the course to the few landmarks she could see. She recognized a point of land looming through the fog on their port side, then a high bridge overhead, and knew they were nearly into the Bay.

Rich came into the galley. He glanced at the compass, then gave Jelly a searching look. "Where to?"

"Sausalito, he tells me."

Rich must have seen the idea hiding behind her eyes. He gave her another long look. "That *is* where you're heading?"

She smiled. But in her mind, she pictured her brother's chart of San Francisco Bay, and the location of the Coast Guard dock.

Lights glimmered on shore. The fog thickened as the sun slid lower in the sky. Jelly remembered a shoal on the port side and directed Redbeard into deeper water. "We're near enough to the Bay," she said. "I think you should make your report."

Buckskin opened the refrigerator and turned dials inside the door. The freezer compartment began to glow. Jelly didn't understand his words when he spoke into the ice tray, but he seemed cheerful. Then the temperature dial spun around like a wheel-of-fortune.

The two girls and Redbeard crowded close to watch. The spinning slowed. The dial came to a stop on the number five. Everyone cheered.

Love gave Jelly a hug. "We have you to thank, River Rat."

"You're not docked, yet," Jelly reminded her. Why did the idea cause a lump in her throat now? She knew it was the right thing to do. The chart of San Francisco Bay was clear in her mind. She peered ahead through the fog.

Billows of mist swirled in every direction. She could hear water washing against a beach as they cruised through Raccoon Strait. She knew the Golden Gate Bridge was somewhere ahead in the fog, but couldn't even see its lights.

She glanced again at the compass. Sausalito was to their right. They would cruise past without even seeing it. She tried to remember where the Coast Guard dock was located on the Bay chart.

Instead, she pictured the girl called Love holding the robin's eggs and crying. The lump in Jelly's throat grew bigger. What would happen when the Coast Guard boarded? She kept hearing Rich saying, "Look at this from their point of view."

She could tell herself they were here to destroy Earth. But did she believe it? Would she ever forget Love's tears? Or the way Buckskin had chided her for wanting to waste a robin's eggs?

Redbeard's voice broke into her thoughts. "Which way, River Rat?"

Jelly hesitated for a full minute longer. "Don't tell anyone I said this," she told him finally. "But maybe you don't have to be born a river rat to be okay." She took a deep breath and let her scheme die. "Turn to starboard, Redbeard. Sausalito is to our right."

The docks of the hillside town began to show through the clinging mist. Jelly felt weak. The thought of heading for the

Coast Guard had filled her with strength. Now . . . well, she could only hope she hadn't made a mistake.

She watched as one boat after another appeared through the fog. But it was Rich who spotted her brother's cruiser. "Hey, Jelly," he called. "Didn't that boat leave The Meadows ahead of us this morning?"

Jelly felt her breath catch in her throat. She turned to Redbeard. "We kept our word. Now it's your turn. That boat over there can take us home."

"You've helped us a lot, River Rat," he said. "Sure would like to keep you with us." He reached over to tousle her hair before turning the spaceboat toward the dock.

Love gave Jelly a hug while Buckskin shook Rich's hand. Feather's eyes filled with tears. "We'll miss you both. Especially you, River Rat."

Jelly felt pleased and embarrassed at the same time. "That's okay," she muttered. She ran out on the deck and waved at Jay as the spaceboat approached.

Her brother was at the stern of his cabin cruiser. He almost dropped his coffee cup when he recognized her. "Jill-Ann! What are you doing on that thing?"

Rich jumped to the dock. Jelly threw him a line before answering Jay. "These are friends of ours. We met them this morning, in The Meadows. They brought us down to join you. We'd better call Mom."

She could see from Jay's face that she had some explaining to do, but it didn't spoil the happiness she felt inside. "Not bad," she called to Rich as he wrapped the spaceboat's line around a cleat on the dock. "You'll be a river rat, yet."

The gangplank banged down and the space crew came through the black door. Jelly introduced them to her brother. He shook hands, with a disbelieving look on his face.

"No offense," he said finally. "But you don't look like my

sister's idea of river boaters."

"Why not?" Jelly demanded. "You should be like me, Jay. Learn to trust people." She grinned at Rich. "City people, hippies . . . and all."

She darted into the cruiser cabin and stopped beside the radio. For a moment, she hesitated. Then she pulled a roll of paper from the chart rack overhead, and ran back to the dock.

"It's for you," she said, handing the roll to Redbeard. "A chart of San Francisco Bay. I know you'll use it well."